Frances Ward Weller

MADAKET MILLIE

illustrated by Marcia Sewall

Philomel Books ◆ New York

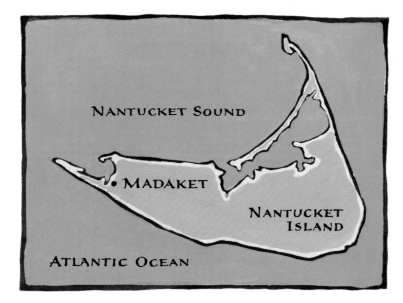

NANTUCKET SOUND

•MADAKET

NANTUCKET
ISLAND

ATLANTIC OCEAN

To Patricia Lee Gauch
author, teacher, editor and friend
who all ways makes a difference.

F.W.W.

For help with research, thanks to Dr. Robert Browning, USCG Historian, and Scott Price of his office; Beverly Hall; Valerie Kincaid, USCG Academy Museum; Eileen P. McGrath, Nantucket Atheneum; Boatswain's Mate Duane Mills, USCG; Jack O'Dell, USCG Office of Media Relations; and Jim Ward, Chief of Community Relations, USCG.

And for memories shared, special thanks to these friends of Millie: George Bassett, Robert C. Caldwell, Frederick C. Coffin, Jr., David Fronzuto, and Dick Whelden (all formerly of the United States Coast Guard); also Amanda Davis and the late Dr. Harlan Davis; Daniel F. and Kathleen Kelliher; Clara Larrabee McGrady; Fred and Joanne Rogers; Annette Stackpole; Sr. Chief David Sweeney, USCG; Elmore Taylor; and the late Sadie Whelden.

Patricia Lee Gauch, Editor.
Text copyright © 1997 by Frances Ward Weller. Illustrations copyright © 1997 by Marcia Sewall. All rights reserved. This book, or parts thereof, may not be reproduced in any form without permission in writing from the publisher, Philomel Books, a division of The Putnam & Grosset Group, 200 Madison Avenue, New York, NY 10016. Philomel Books, Reg. U.S. Pat. & Tm. Off. Published simultaneously in Canada. Printed in Singapore. Book design by Gunta Alexander. The text is set in Palatino. Library of Congress Cataloging-in-Publication Data.
Weller, Frances Ward. Madaket Millie/Frances Ward Weller; illustrated by Marcia Sewall. p. cm. Summary: After the Coasties close the Madaket Station on Nantucket Island, Millie appoints herself warden, rescue squad, and sentry providing lifesaving services along the coast. [1. Islands—Fiction. 2. Lifesaving—Fiction. 3. Rescue work—Fiction. 4. Nantucket Island (Mass.)—Fiction.] I. Sewall, Marcia, ill. II. Title. PZ7.W454Mad. 1997. [E]—dc20 95-17058 CIP AC
ISBN 0-399-22785-7 (hc) 10 9 8 7 6 5 4 3 2 1 First Impression

AUTHOR'S NOTE

Mildred Jewett was larger than life, hard to pare and pummel into the confines of this book. Besides, beneath the crusty surface of the legend, I found surprising soft spots, sorrows, and little mysteries. Did Millie hate the word "goodbye" because it had come too finally and too often—from her mother, from her brother, who migrated to Alaska for life, and from her mail-order husband, who went off to war and never came back? Did she insist on the Native American spelling of "Maddaquet" because the Wampanoags' meaning— "Bad Lands"—suited her own hard and lonely life? And how could such a prickly person be so profoundly caring?

What's certain is that Millie was born in Nantucket town on September 24, 1907, and died on March 1, 1990. That the times she left her island could probably be counted on the fingers of one hand. That for more than half a century, her exploits and eccentricity were vivid strands in the fabric of Nantucket life. That though she relished recognition by her beloved Coast Guard, she was a reluctant celebrity, not fond of being a Nantucket sight-to-see. That she loved animals, books, coffee ice cream, and people without pretense—who were often children.

Millie lived all the life she could remember in Madaket, that windy ocean edge of Nantucket Island. She was tiny when her mother left, never to return, and her silent father took her to live on her grandmother's farm. Life there was beautiful, but hard and chancy. Villagers clung to the island's corner, fishing and farming. Only a rumpled ribbon of dirt road threaded the moors toward town.

"But, never mind, child," Millie's Gram said briskly. "Where life has set you, make a difference!"

The ocean drummed the rhythm of Millie's
life, thundering onto Madaket Beach, sighing
in tides that turned in Hither Creek and harbor.
Through summers, springs and falls, Millie
tended crops and critters, and combed the
beach for driftwood.

Winters, the men of Madaket chugged to
the bays for scallops and brought them back by
bushels. Millie was a whiz at scallop shucking.
So while town children sat at proper desks in a
proper school, Millie stood at a scallop bench
with Gram reading to her.

Island firesides rang with tales of shipwreck and adventure. But Millie herself saw the ocean rise from calm to fury, and knew it needed to be watched and understood.

At the lifesaving station atop the dunes, the Coast Guard men stood watch. When Millie brought them good farm vegetables, she stayed to climb the lookout's stairs or drink in songs and rescue stories.

She knew the Coasties understood the sea. They walked the outer beaches in all weather and shot their boats through walls of surf to help seafarers in distress.

Millie's head said there were no women in the lifesaving service, but her heart said, "Why not?" So when work was done, she clambered up the farmhouse roof to watch the sea.

She hefted bigger bags of scallops. She practiced knots and mastered a dory alone. As she grew up she came to know each stretch of shore and every boat and boater in the harbor.

Meanwhile she farmed and shucked and tried her hand at plumbing. She built an ice cream stand for summer folks and ran from task to task, or flew on horseback like a cowboy, chaps flapping in the wind. For years she was the idol of the neighbor boys.

Then a great war flared across the sea, and the Coast Guard began to enlist women.

Millie rushed to volunteer. "Your eyes don't measure up," the Coast Guard told her. But she learned they needed dogs trained to patrol the beaches. "They can't keep me from doin' that!" muttered Millie.

By war's end, she had taught a score of furry recruits to come, stay, sit, heel, crawl, and climb.

What's more, she'd taught the Coast Guard just how strong was Millie Jewett. On the beach one day, she elbowed past four Coasties struggling with a driftwood giant.

"Stand back," barked Millie, "and let an Islander try!" With two deft moves, she had three hundred pounds of log upon her shoulders, bound for home.

The grateful Coast Guard gave her honorary rank, and Millie felt she might truly belong. But then she heard Madaket Station would be closed. Fancy new ways of tracking ships meant patrols along the beach weren't needed.

"Not so!" said Millie, for all her life she'd known these winds and shoals. Trouble came fast, and being there was half the battle.

But no one listened. The last Madaket surfmen shuttered the tower windows and took their boats to harbor in Nantucket town.

That very night, Millie marched up her favorite dune, raised her binoculars, and found lights up the beach where none should be. Confused by fog, a giant freighter was aground. Millie raced for home. At her call, rescue boats came swarming.

That decided Millie. She'd patrol the shore each day at first and last light. Where life had set her, she would make a difference.

"I'll help anyone I can," she said, "if it's two in the afternoon or two in the morning."

So it was Millie who rowed clear across the harbor at sunset to help boaters becalmed. It was Millie who knew when a neighbor fisherman was late returning to his mooring, Millie who ran the lanes of Madaket calling his family and every fisherman she knew to find the reason why.

And it was Millie who went to battle with the shark washed into Hither Creek by storm one October day—Millie, flexing burly arms, who rowed and pitchforked until the shark was beached.

"Just a day's job," said Millie.

In summer fog and winter gale, Millie was warden, rescue squad, and sentry on the beat. "She never sleeps," the Coasties said. Sure as the tide, Millie was always, always there.

No wonder she had little time for things that wouldn't make a difference. She sold her land and teetering farmhouse to a man who built her a spanking new scallop shed and cottage by the creek, with a promise she could live there the rest of her days.

Her friends and neighbors rejoiced and hung up starchy curtains. But they might have known Millie would make the place homey in her own way, with swarms of barking dogs and begging ducks and anchors in the bathtub.

She never felt a call to clean her snug new home. She filled it up with towers of blankets, cans and slickers for emergencies, but kept a path cleared to the bed she slept in with her biggest, warmest dog for company.

"If you need someone to talk to in the middle of the night," Millie explained, "a dog will always listen."

What mattered was, hers was the perfect spot for watching over Madaket—hard by Hither Creek, commanding bridge and road and harbor. So Millie didn't care about the hums of her new TV, pipes and furnace. She listened for the pulse of passing boats, the phone and crackling CB radio. Those were her lookouts, often swifter than the Coast Guard's fancy gear.

They told her when a charter boat was swamped off shore. Millie mustered sloops, cruisers and scallop boats to pluck survivors from a sea that tried to swallow them.

When a sailboat ran aground one summer morning, Millie phoned the Coast Guard. "*Shearwater*'s beached on Tuckernuck," she told them. "Ha, how'd I find her? Two outbound fishermen and Jimmy Folger's barkin' dog."

Millie was there when hurricanes screamed toward Nantucket and people had to leave most seaside places. "Can't we ride out the storm?" some neighbors pleaded. In Madaket, the call was left to Millie. Sometimes she cast a weather eye about and sent them packing. Most times, she helped them batten down.

"You stay," said Millie. "I'll take care of you."

She rarely left her corner of Nantucket and never dreamed of fame. Yet Millie stories spread till every schoolchild, scalloper, cook, librarian, carpenter, lawyer, and shopkeeper—every islander on land and sea—knew Millie Jewett.

Some were proud to call her friend, and some were wary of this prickly woman. But every year more of the summer pilgrims coming 'round the point sought out a glimpse of Millie.

The Coast Guard even said she could fly weather flags for boaters. "That's good," said Millie, running red gale warning pennants up her pole. "But I decide when to put 'em up and I decide when to take 'em down." Millie always did make her own rules.

At last they hung a sign with Coast Guard chevrons above her cottage door. The sign read, "United States Coast Guard, Nantucket, West End Command."

"Well," she chuckled, "it's about time!"

It wasn't clear who had adopted whom, but ever after the United States Coast Guard was Millie's family. Each Tuesday, standing tall so's not to muss her uniform, Millie waited for the Coast Guard truck she rode to market and on to Brant Point to inspect the troops.

"Button that pocket and polish those buttons," she'd bark. "You're a Coastie! Be proud of it!"

Good-byes were hard to say when Millie died. For fourscore years she'd made a difference in Madaket, as constant as a star and sturdy as a harbor piling.

She'd have loved the Coast Guard's tribute on her shore, an honor guard and a copter drifting her ashes over Hither Creek.

She'd have liked the new sign with her name that marks the bridge. But nowadays she wouldn't know West End Command: no barking dogs, no mound of scallop shells, no ducklings in the bathtub.

A quarterboard still says the place is Millie's. But no one's there to raise the storm flags on the empty pole. No one to say, "You stay. I'll take care of you." What's Millie's still are water, wind, and sky, and a place in Island storying, so long as Hither Creek runs to the sea.